DISCARD

**First published in the United States 1989
by Chronicle Books**

Text copyright © 1987 by Ulf Nilsson
Illustrations copyright © 1987 by Eva Eriksson

First published in Sweden 1987 by Bonniers
Printed in Denmark
Library of Congress
Cataloging-in-Publication Data

Nilsson, Ulf, 1948-
  Little Bunny & the Hungry Fox.
  [När lilla syster Kanin blev jagad av en räv.
English]
  Little Bunny takes a walk / Ulf Nilsson,
Eva Eriksson.
    p. cm.
  Translation of: När lilla syster Kanin blev
jagad av en räv.
  Summary: Little Bunny's relaxing walk
is interrupted by a hungry fox.
  ISBN 0-87701-605-4:
  [1. Rabbits–Fiction. 2. Foxes–Fiction.]
I. Eriksson, Eva. II. Title.
PZ7.N589Lh 1989
[E]–dc19   88-30848
                                        CIP
Distributed in Canada by   AC
Raincoast Books
112 East Third Avenue
Vancouver, B.C.
V5T 1C8

10 9 8 7 6 5 4 3 2 1

Chronicle Books
275 Fifth Street
San Francisco, California 94103

Little Bunny
& the Hungry Fox

Ulf Nilsson ❦ Eva Eriksson

Chronicle Books
San Francisco

Little Bunny peeked out her doorway.
"Nice day for a walk," she thought.

Mama Rabbit had warned her not to go out by herself.

"But I'll only be gone a minute," thought Little Bunny.

And off she went.

She whistled a little song.

She somersaulted down a hill.

Then she stopped to pick some flowers.

"Is there something hiding in the bushes?" she wondered.

There was! It was a hungry fox.

Little Bunny was so surprised, she dropped her flowers.

Sniff, sniff, sniff went the fox.

Little Bunny didn't know what to do, so she just stood perfectly still.

"Hop!" squawked the birds as they flew into the air.

But Little Bunny didn't see them.

All she could see was the fox.

"Hop!" squawked the birds again.

But Little Bunny didn't hear them.

All she could hear was the fox saying, "Yum. Yum. Yum."

"HOP!" squawked the birds.

Finally Little Bunny did just that.

She hopped high into the air.   The hungry fox was startled.

Little Bunny hopped over a bush. She hopped over a rock.

The hungry fox tried hard to follow.

Little Bunny hopped up a hill. She hopped back down.

The hungry fox was getting tired.

Little Bunny hopped as fast as she could across a field.

Finally, the hungry fox could run no more.

Little Bunny hopped happily down the road.

Then she hop-hop-hopped all the way home.